Wings

SHINSUKE TANAKA

Purple Bear Books · New York

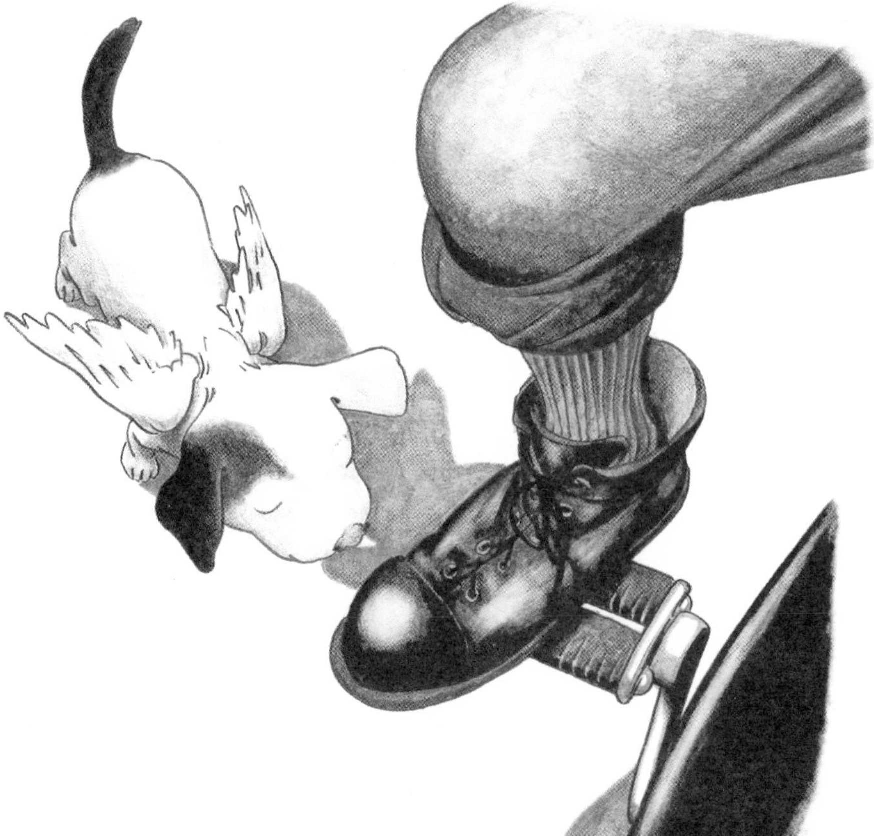

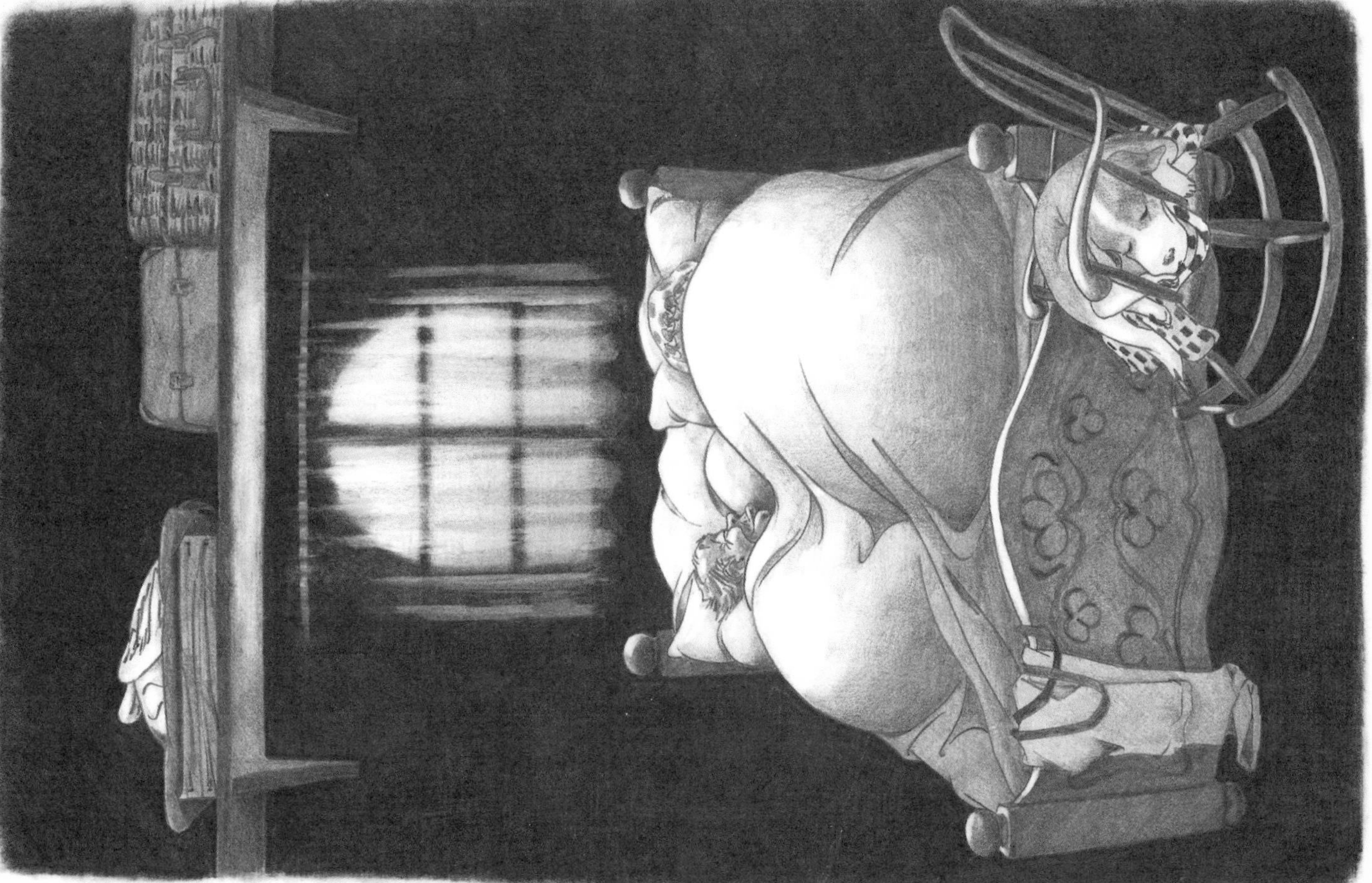

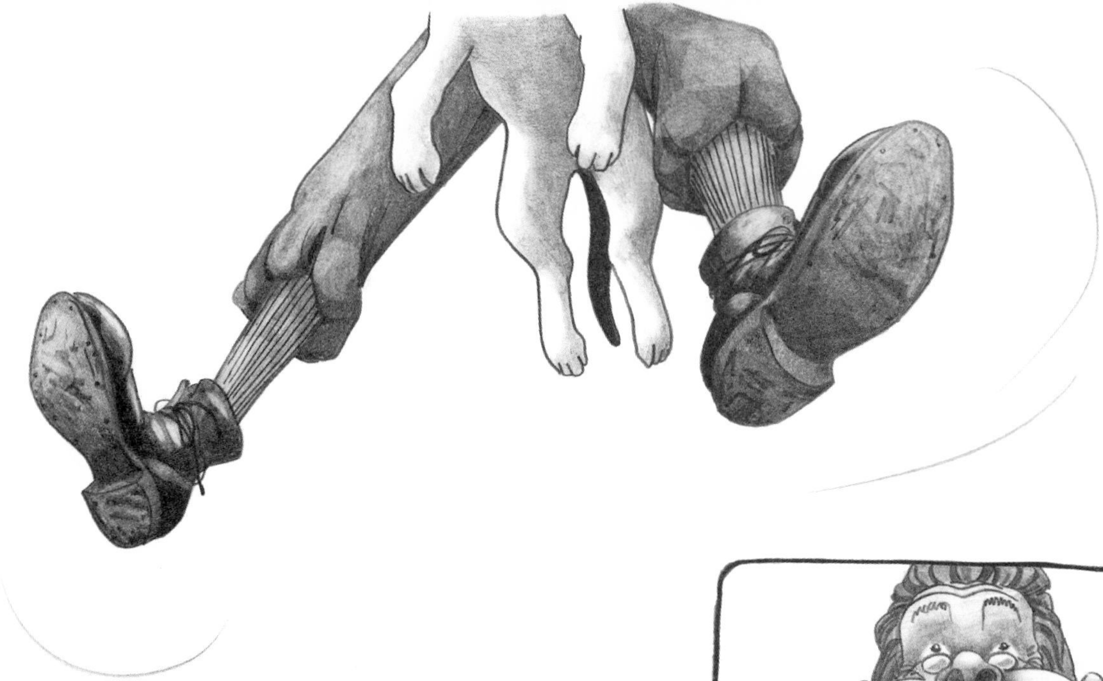

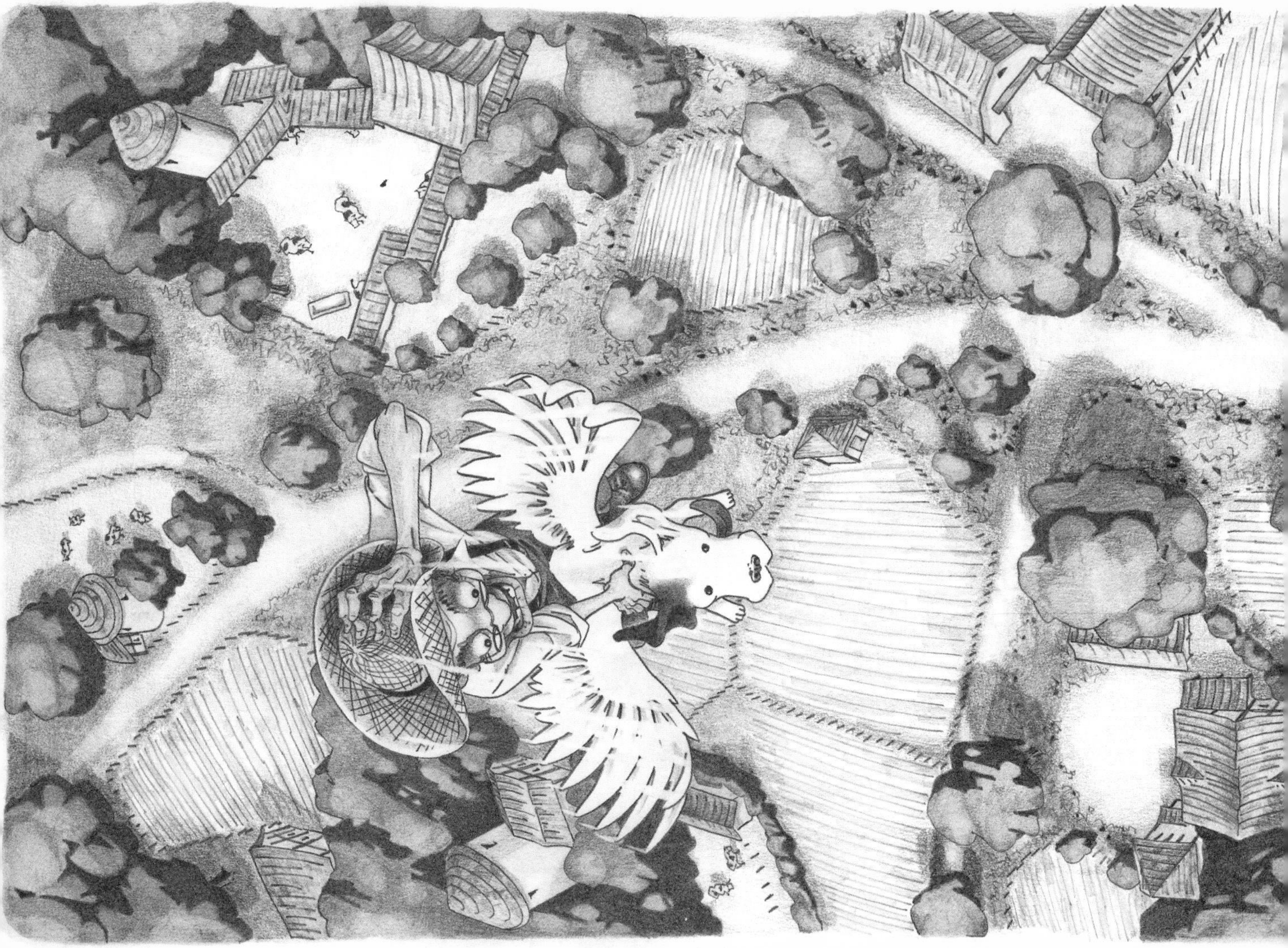

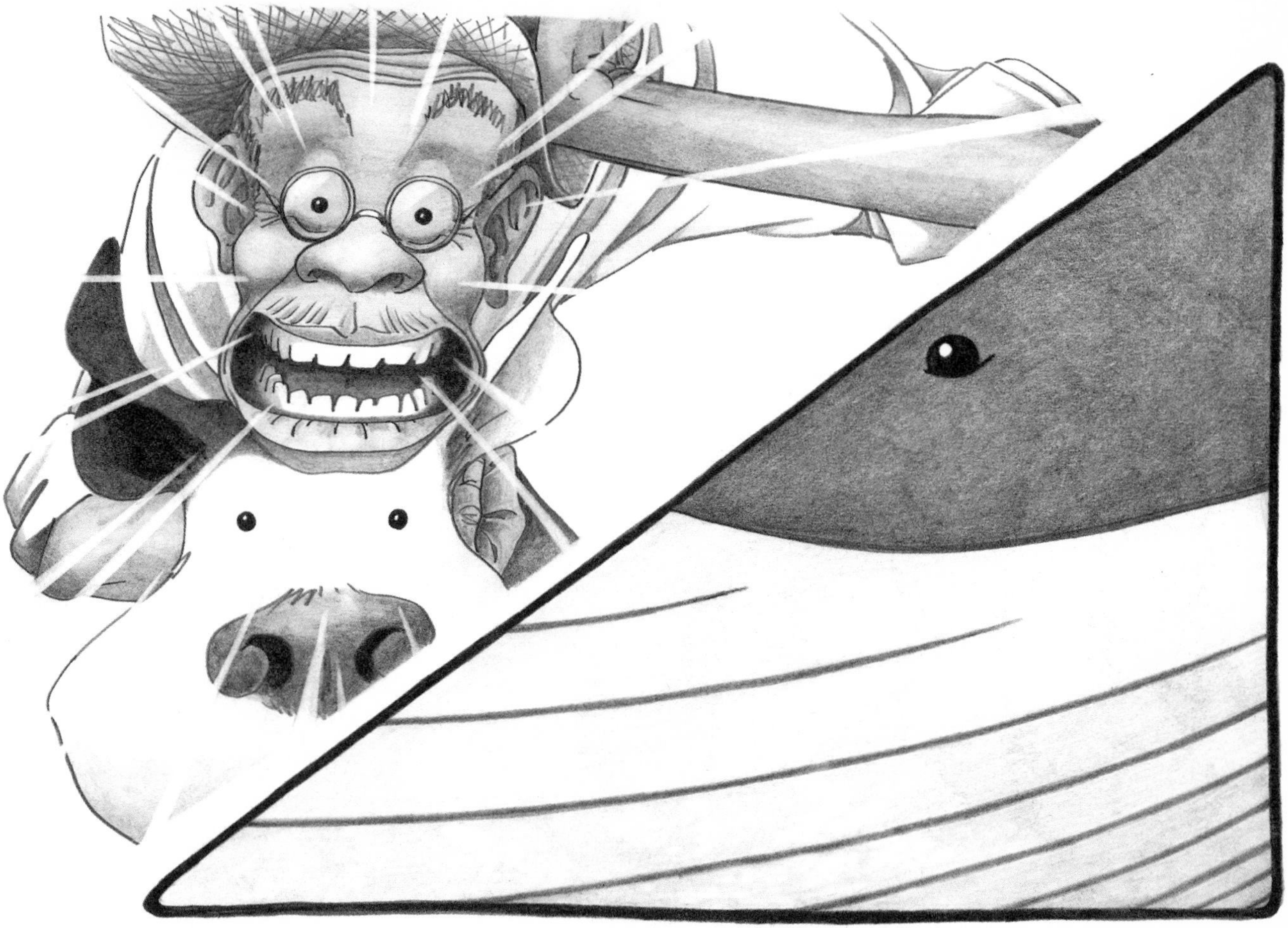

POST OFFICE

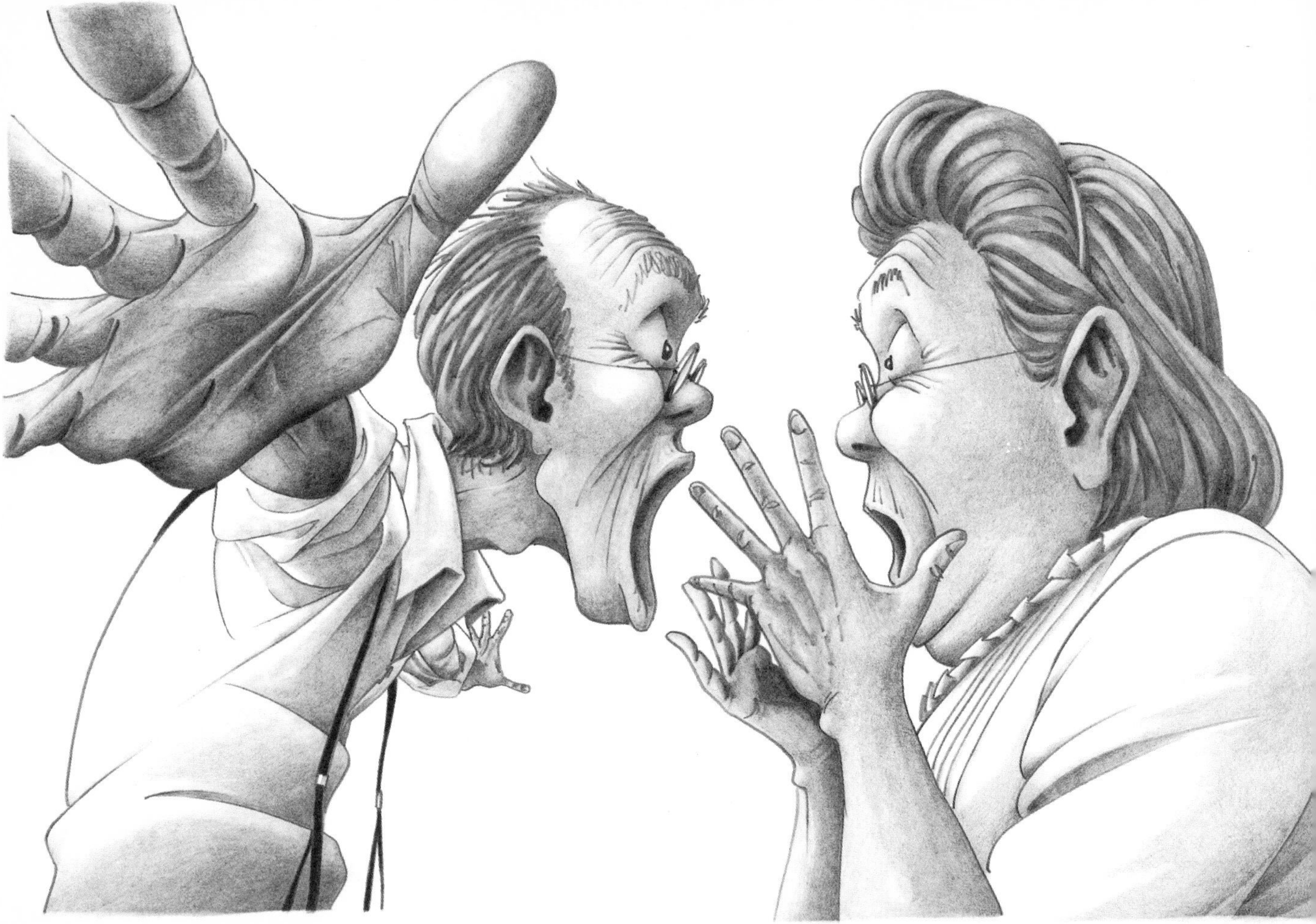

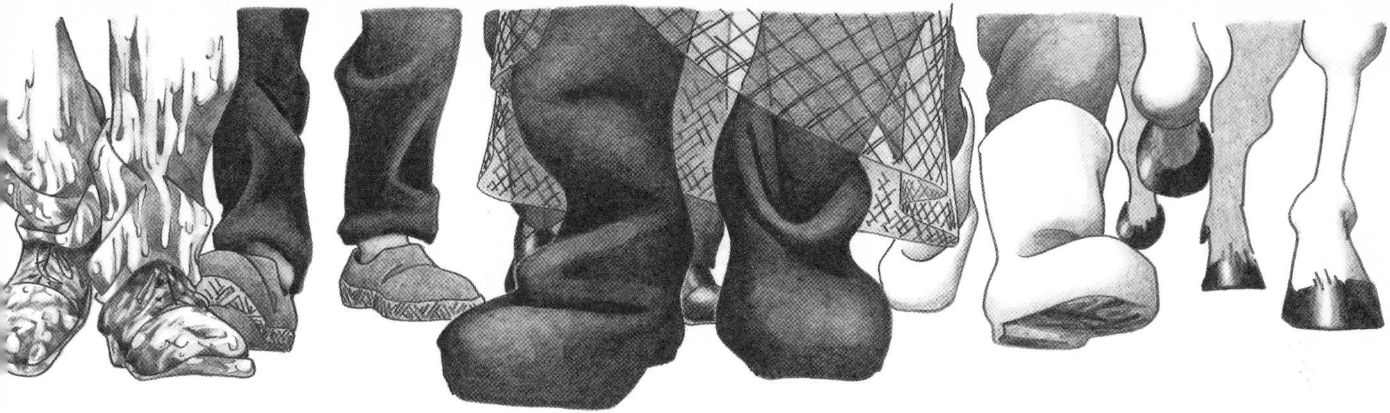

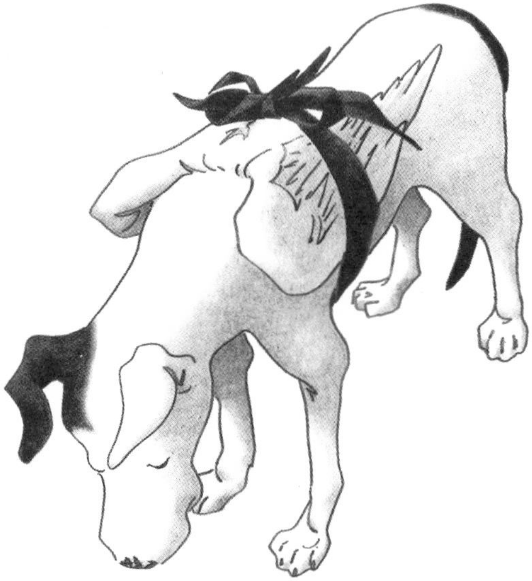

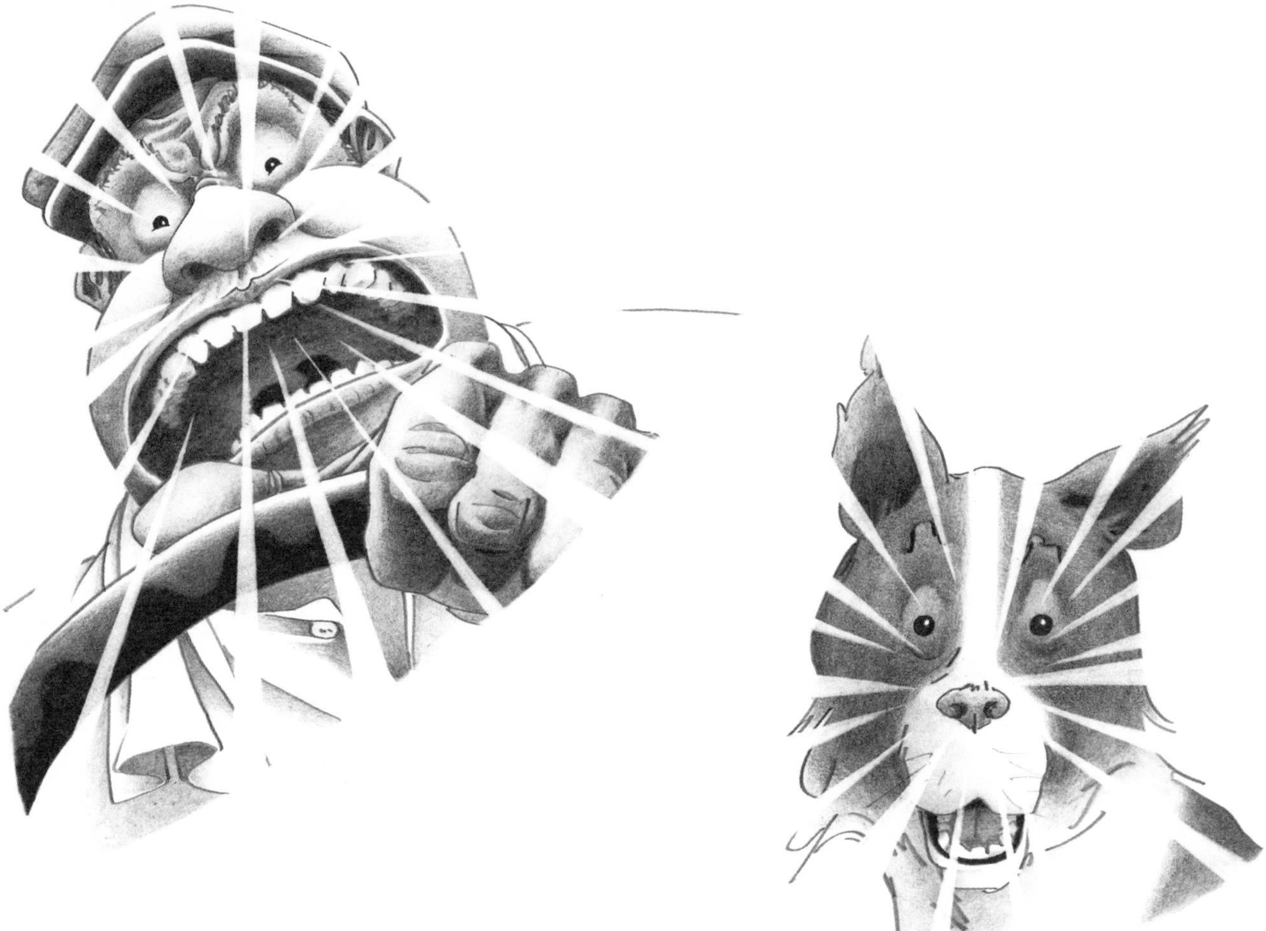

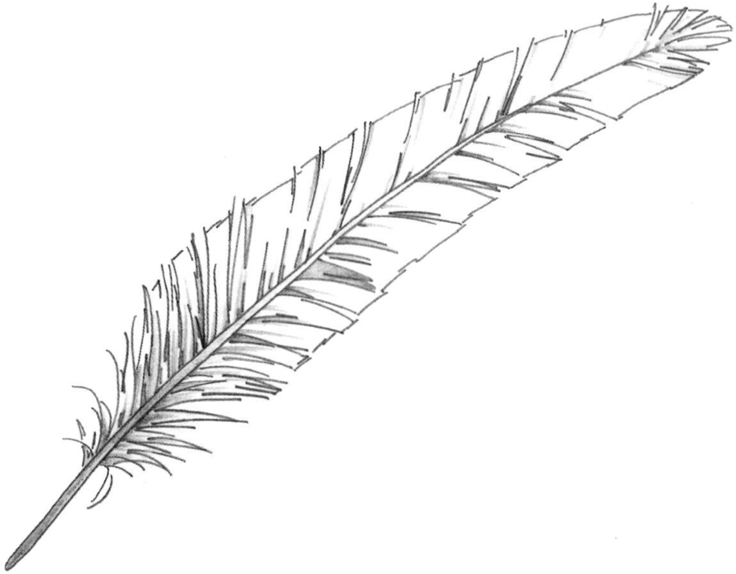

First English-language edition published in 2006 by Purple Bear Books Inc., New York

by arrangement with Grimm Press, Taiwan.

For more information about our books, visit our website: purplebearbooks.com

Library of Congress Cataloging-in-Publication Data is available.

This edition prepared by Cheshire Studio.

ISBN-10: 1-933327-19-7

ISBN-13: 978-1-933327-19-8

1 3 5 7 9 10 8 6 4 2

Printed in Taiwan